STECK-V

NEW

LEARNING WITH LITERATURE

Tom Gets Fit
and
Other Stories

Illustrated by Nina O'Connell

CONTENTS

STECK-VAUGHN
COMPANY

Tom Gets Fit

"Tom, you must get fit.
You need to run,"
said Ben.

"Tom, you must get fit.

You need to jump,"

said Meg.

"Tom, you must get fit.

You need to hop,"

said Deb.

"Tom, you must get fit.
You need to bend,"
said Jip.

"Look at me,"
said Tom.
"I will get fit."

What's for Lunch?

"I will buy some

jam for Jip," said Tom.

"I will see if it is good."

So he did.

"I will buy some
milk for Deb," said Tom.
"I will see if it is good."
So he did.

"I will buy some
buns for Ben," said Tom.
"I will see if they are good."
So he did.

"I will buy some
meat for Sam," said Tom.
"I will see if it is good."
So he did.

I will make a good lunch
for Jip, Deb, Ben, and Sam.
And he did.

A Healthy Visit

Tom was sad.

He was in bed.

He had a cold.

Ben went to see Tom.

"Here is a bone," said Ben.

Sam went to see Tom.

"Here is a cake," said Sam.

"Thank you, thank you,"
said Tom.

You make me feel better!